First published in the United States, Great Britain, Canada,
Australia and New Zealand in 1990 by North-South Books,
an imprint of Rada Matija AG, 8625 Gossau ZH, Switzerland.

Library of Congress Catalog Card Number: 89-43248
Library of Congress Cataloging in Publication Data is available.
ISBN 1-55858-087-5

British Library Cataloguing in Publication Data
Ostheeren, Ingrid
Jonathan Mouse and the magic box.
I. Title II. Mathieu, Agnès, *1956-* III. Jonathan die
Zaubermaus. *English*
833.'914 [J]

ISBN 1-55858-087-5

1   3   5   7   9   10   8   6   4   2

Printed in Germany

Jonathan Mouse
and the Magic Box

By Ingrid Ostheeren
Illustrated by Agnès Mathieu
Translated by Rosemary Lanning

North-South Books
New York

One fine summer's day Jonathan, the mischievous little mouse, was walking down the hill toward the farmhouse.

He had just eaten a delicious meal, yet for once he was not at all sleepy. Since he had nothing important to do and was very bored, he decided to sneak into the farmhouse and explore the attic.

As he scampered up the stairs, Jonathan could see that the attic was very dark. Two small windows in the roof let in just a little bit of light.

Jonathan rummaged inquisitively through all the nooks and crannies. The most interesting thing he found was a basket filled with dusty old books and a strange-looking hat covered with stars. Although Jonathan couldn't have known it, everything in the basket had once belonged to the farmer's great-great-grandfather, a mysterious man who claimed to be a wizard.

At the bottom of the basket, Jonathan discovered a small, round box. He pulled it out and tried to open it, but the lid was stuck tight. He kept on pulling and tugging until suddenly the lid sprang off and a fine silver powder flew into the air.

"How boring." muttered Jonathan as the powder showered over him and covered his fur. "I wish this could have been filled with cheese."

All at once the attic was full of the pungent smell of ripe cheese. Sitting right next to the basket was the biggest stack of cheese Jonathan had ever seen!

"I'm a wizard!" he shouted, jumping up off the floor. "This must be a magic box! Full of magic dust!"

Jonathan was so excited that he ignored the cheese, ran across the attic, down the stairs and out into the farmyard.

The first things he saw were the pigs jostling around their trough, grunting and smacking their lips.

"Greedy things," said Jonathan as a grin spread across his face. "They never share their food with me. What fun can I have with them? I know. I'll make them fly!"

Jonathan pointed at the pigs and said, "Hocus-pocus, up you go!" Slowly the pigs rose into the air and flew around the farmyard, squeaking anxiously. When the farm dog saw the flying pigs he went wild and his barking brought the dairymaid to the window of the house.

"Oh no!" she cried. "I don't believe it! Flying pigs! What is the farmer's wife going to say when she comes home from the market?"

Jonathan giggled with glee. "This is fun!" he shouted.

He turned to the cows, who were peering over the fence at the strange sight in the farmyard.

Jonathan pointed at them and said, "Dance, cows! Dance and sing! That is the wish of Jonathan, the Wizard. Abracadabra. Hey presto!"

With that, the cows rose up on their hind legs and began to dance and sing.

Then Jonathan caught sight of the rooster and the hens, who were pecking around in the yard. "We need music and you shall make it," he announced. "And our friend the dog can be the conductor. Hocus-pocus. Alacazam!"

Next he made the goats do handstands and the pony juggle cabbages. Then he paused to watch the fun while he decided what to do with the ducks on the pond.

Jonathan laughed so hard that he started to cry. He had just turned the little ducks into huge hippos who were struggling to fit into the small pond. Behind him, the dairymaid couldn't believe what she was seeing.

At the sight of the chicken orchestra she shrieked. When she saw the acrobatic goats and the juggling pony she shook her head in despair. Now the pond was filled with strange creatures and there was a mouse rolling on the ground, howling with laughter. "The whole farm has gone mad!" she cried.

But then she saw something so normal that she rubbed her eyes in disbelief. Creeping quietly across the yard was a cat. He was even behaving like a cat since he was heading straight for the laughing mouse.

Because he was laughing so hard at his wonderful tricks, Jonathan didn't notice the cat. Luckily, the dairymaid shouted, "Leave the poor mouse alone—he's gone mad!"

Jonathan saw the cat just in time, jumped up, ran straight toward the pond and plunged bravely into the heap of hippos. He climbed over the huge animals and clambered back onto dry land on the far side of the pond. He shook himself quickly and ran toward the house.

As he ran, something strange happened. All the magic stopped. The water had washed the powder off his fur.

The cows had gone back to munching grass. The dog lay sleepily in front of his kennel. The hens were scratching for food and the five little ducks swam happily on the pond.

When the farmer's wife drove her cart into the farmyard, the dairymaid ran out to meet her.

"I'm so glad to see you!" said the dairymaid. "Someone has cast a spell on all the animals!"

As they walked into the house, the farmer's wife listened patiently to the dairymaid's story.

Jonathan watched as the farmer's wife shook her head and said, "Flying pigs? Dancing cows? Such things are impossible, my dear. You've been working too hard. Come into the kitchen and let me make you some tea."

A mischievous grin spread across Jonathan's little face. He looked at the delicious cake sitting in front of him and said, "The magic powder may have washed off, but I can still make this cake disappear!"